From the Author, Stacey Goodwin

For Lucian's spirit.
For Colin's heart.
For Addison's love.

From the Illustrator, Nicolas Ceasar

To Jones.
And the memory of Boo, RIP.

From the Designer, Jessica Lyonford

For my amazing sisters
who are changing the world
with their hearts.

Printed by CreateSpace, An Amazon.com Company
First printing, 2018.

Sometimes I'm Sorry

Sometimes I'm sorry and
I don't know why.

I sit in my bedroom
and maybe I cry.

I'm acting one way
I'd rather not be

Please.
Don't ever.
Touch me.

I feel pins in my skin.

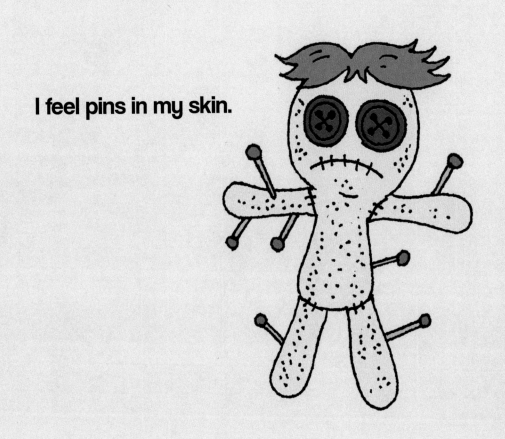

I can hardly breathe.

Can everyone please just stop looking at me?!

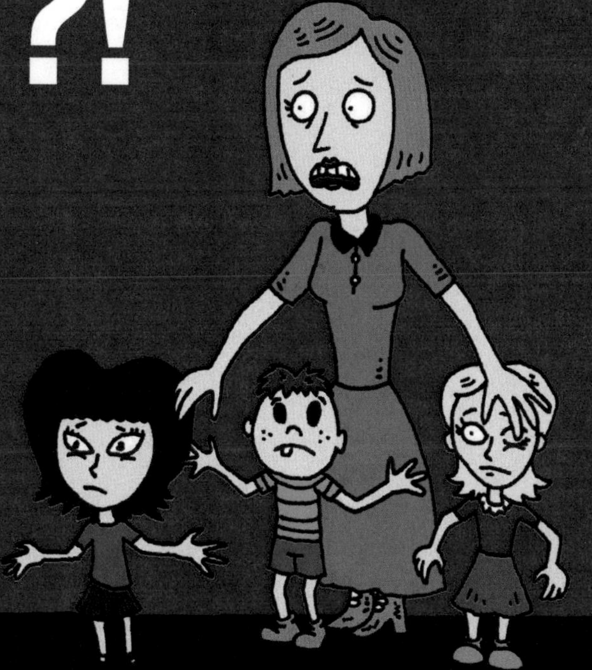

There are people around.
They don't mean to stare.

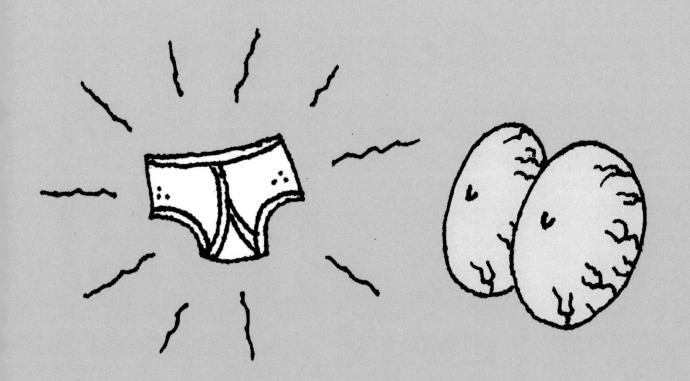

They can't actually see my underwear.

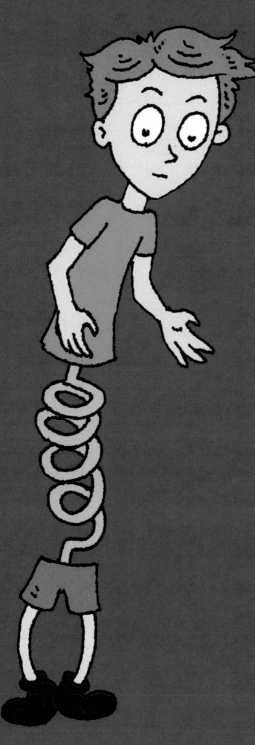

Maybe they are trying to help me unwind.

That place I am going, one day I'll find.

Uphill, I see.

I see.

I see.

That battle you face
may not actually
be quite as scary
as you let it be.

It's okay to feel
often.

It's okay to feel
odd.

Sometimes your feelings
may seem locked somewhere far.

It's okay to be mad   and you can be blue.

But please remember
that you are loved, too.

The End

Made in the USA
Middletown, DE
28 August 2022

72547599R00018